The L... ...d Hen

A Publication of the World Language Division

Director of Product Development: Judith M. Bittinger

Executive Editor: Elinor Chamas

Editorial Development: Elly Schottman

Production/Manufacturing: James W. Gibbons

Cover and Text Design/Art Direction: Taurins Design Associates, New York

Illustrator: Jerry Smath

ISBN 0-201-19364-7

30 31 32 33 34 35-PX-08 07 06 05

Addison-Wesley Publishing Company

Once upon a time,
there was a busy
little red hen.

She lived on a farm with
a lazy duck, a lazy cat,
and a lazy dog.

"Who will help me
    plant this wheat?"
asked the Little Red Hen.

"Not I!" said the duck.
"Not I!" said the cat.
"Not I!" said the dog.

"Then I will do it myself,"
    said the Little Red Hen.

And she did.

5

"Who will help me
cut the wheat?"
asked the Little Red Hen.

"Not I!" said the duck.
"Not I!" said the cat.
"Not I!" said the dog.

"Then I will do it myself,"
said the Little Red Hen.

And she did.

"Who will help me
make the flour?"
asked the Little Red Hen.

"Not I!" said the duck.
"Not I!" said the cat.
"Not I!" said the dog.

"Then I will do it myself,"
said the Little Red Hen.

And she did.

9

"Who will help me
make the bread?"
asked the Little Red Hen.

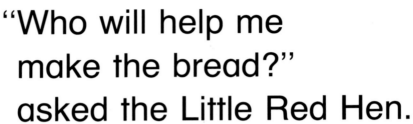

"Not I!" said the duck.
"Not I!" said the cat.
"Not I!" said the dog.

"Then I will do it myself,"
said the Little Red Hen.

And she did.

11

"Who will help me
eat the bread?"
asked the Little Red Hen.

I will!" said the duck.
I will!" said the cat.
I will!" said the dog.

13

"No, you won't,"
 said the Little Red Hen.

14

"I made it myself
and I'll eat it myself."

And she did.

The End